IF FOUND, PLEASE

RETURN TO:

_____

_____

_____

_____

THE
DaVinci
CODE *travel journal*

Based on the novel by

DAN BROWN

POTTER STYLE

Bourbon S.t

Lumiverte S.t

Varenne

se H.

Seine R

A PLAN of
the CITY of
PARIS.

tal
se H.

Hotel

A list of credits appears on page 160.

Copyright © 2006 by Dan Brown
All rights reserved. All excerpts are used by permission of Dan Brown.
Published in the United States by Clarkson Potter/Publishers, an imprint of Crown
Publishing Group, a division of Random House, Inc.
www.crownpublishing.com
www.clarksonpotter.com

Based on *The Da Vinci Code* by Dan Brown, published in 2003 by Doubleday,
a division of Random House, Inc.

Clarkson Potter, Potter Style, and colophon are trademarks of Random House, Inc.

ISBN-13: 978-0-307-34576-9
ISBN-10: 0-307-34576-9

Cover design by Jan Derevjanik
Interior design by Jan Derevjanik and Patrice Sheridan

Printed in China

10 9 8 7 6 5 4 3 2 1

First Edition

LET THE JOURNEY BEGIN . . .

Millions of readers have been captivated by the epic journey that Robert Langdon and Sophie Neveu undertake to solve the mysteries presented in *The Da Vinci Code*. In fact, the novel has inspired countless travel itineraries, ranging from neighborhood walking tours to three-week voyages across Europe. Whether you're about to embark on a major quest or gradually visit the locations described in the book over time, this travel journal is designed for capturing your firsthand impressions of *The Da Vinci Code* phenomenon.

Bon Voyage!

the DA VINCI CODE
itinerary

Paris

ROBERT LANGDON'S ROUTE THROUGH PARIS (MAP)
  The Hotel Ritz Paris
  The Eiffel Tower
  Tuileries Gardens
  Arc du Carrousel (and surrounding museums)

THE SCENE OF THE CRIME: MUSÉE DU LOUVRE
  La Pyramide
  The Mona Lisa
  Madonna of the Rocks

LANGDON AND NEVEU'S ESCAPE FROM THE LOUVRE
  Arc de Triomphe and the Champs-Elysées
  Gare Saint-Lazare
  Bois de Boulogne

SILAS FOLLOWS A FALSE CLUE
  The Church of Saint-Sulpice

THE GRAIL QUEST CONTINUES WITH SIR LEIGH TEABING
  Château Villette

THE TRUE RESTING PLACE OF THE GRAIL? (MAP)
  Langdon's Epilogue Discovery

London

Edinburgh

Subplots and Side Trips

PARIS

Robert Langdon awoke slowly.

A telephone was ringing in the darkness—a tinny, unfamiliar ring. He fumbled for the bedside lamp and turned it on. Squinting at his surroundings he saw a plush Renaissance bedroom with Louis XVI furniture, hand-frescoed walls, and a colossal mahogany four-poster bed.

Where the hell am I?

The jacquard bathrobe hanging on his bedpost bore the monogram:

HOTEL RITZ PARIS

PARIS

Robert Langdon awoke slowly.

A telephone was ringing in the darkness—a tinny, unfamiliar ring. He fumbled for the bedside lamp and turned it on. Squinting at his surroundings he saw a plush Renaissance bedroom with Louis XVI furniture, hand-frescoed walls, and a colossal mahogany four-poster bed.

Where the hell am I?

The jacquard bathrobe hanging on his bedpost bore the monogram:

HOTEL RITZ PARIS

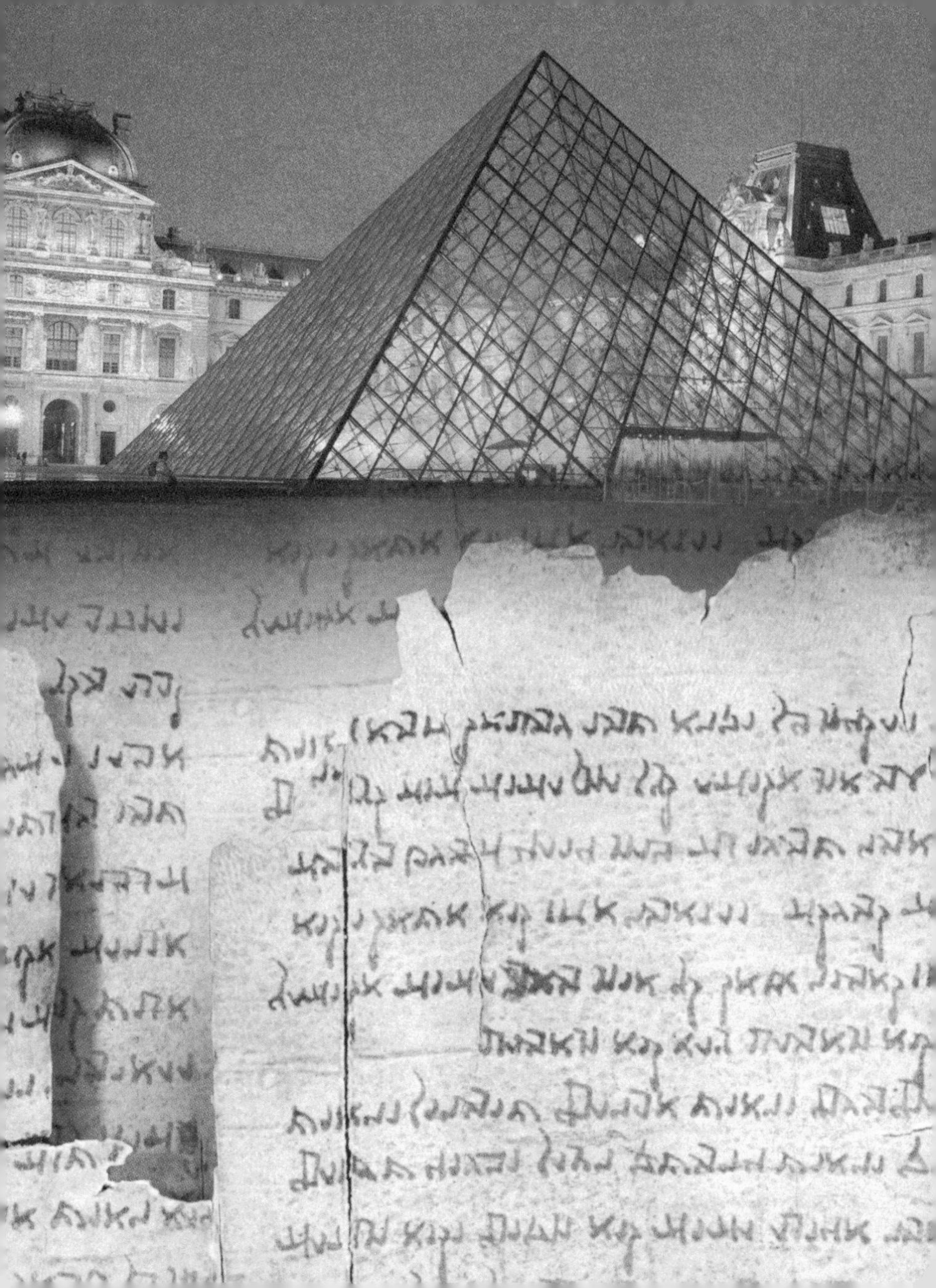

PARIS

FRANCE

Sacré Coeur ①

MONTMART

PIGALLE ⑫

Bd. de Clichy

⑪

Gare St-Lazare

Opéra

La Madeleine

Pavillon Dauphine ◆

Arc de Triomphe ⑩

Hotel Ritz Paris ①

Bois de Boulogne ⑭

Grand Palais

Petit Palais

Musé du Jeu de Paume

Pl. de la Concorde

Jardin des Tuileries

Palais Royal

Louvre ⑧

SEE INSET BELOW LEFT

Palais de Chaillot

Tour Eiffel ②

American University of Paris ◆

Musée d'Orsay ⑤

Quai Voltaire

Hôtel des Invalides

ST-GERMAIN DES PRÉS

St-Sulpice ⑮

QUAI

Ecole Militaire

Palais du Luxembourg

Jardin du Luxembourg

Sor

Pant

AUTEUIL

Gare Montparnasse

Cimetière du Montparnasse

L'Observatoire de Paris ◆

Parc Montsouris

MONTROUGE

Cité Universitaire

GENT

Inset (below left)

Hotel de Crillon ◆

U.S. Embassy ◆

Pl. Vendôme

Palais Royal ◆

Musée du Jeu de Paume

⑦

Pl. de la Concorde

Jardin des Tuileries ③

Seine

Louvre

Comédie-Française

Jardin de Palais Royal

Arc du Carrousel ④

⑨ La Pyramide

Musée d'Orsay ◆

Quai Voltaire

Pont du Carrousel ◆

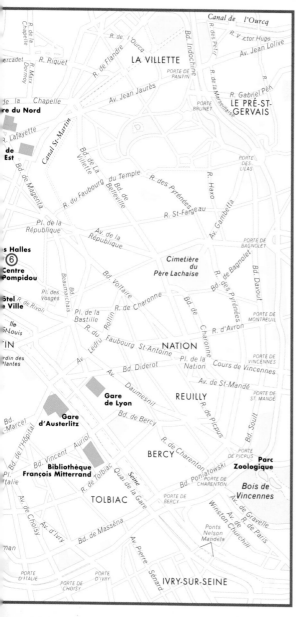

EIFFEL TOWER ②

"She is lovely, no?" The agent motioned through the windshield toward the Eiffel Tower.

. . .

"She is the symbol of France. I think she is perfect."

Langdon nodded absently. Symbologists often remarked that France—a country renowned for machismo, womanizing, and diminutive insecure leaders like Napoleon and Pepin the Short—could not have chosen a more apt national emblem than a thousand-foot phallus.

your photo of the
Eiffel Towel here

TUILERIES
GARDENS ③

The agent gunned the sedan across
the junction and sped onto a
wooded section of Rue Castiglione,
which served as the northern
entrance to the famed Tuileries
Gardens—Paris's own version of
Central Park.

. . .

Langdon had always considered the
Tuileries to be sacred ground.
These were the gardens in which
Claude Monet had experimented
with form and color, and literally
inspired the birth of the Impres-
sionist movement. Tonight, however, this place held a strange aura of
foreboding.

Arc du Carrousel ④

Despite the orgiastic rituals once held at the Arc du Carrousel, art aficionados revered this place for another reason entirely. From the esplanade at the end of the Tuileries, four of the finest art museums in the world could be seen . . . one at each point of the compass.

Out the right-hand window, south across the Seine and Quai Voltaire, Langdon could see the dramatically lit facade of the old train station—now the esteemed **Musée d'Orsay** ⑤. Glancing left, he could make out the top of the ultramodern **Pompidou Center** ⑥, which housed the Museum of Modern Art. Behind him to the west, Langdon knew the ancient obelisk of Ramses rose above the trees, marking the **Musée du Jeu de Paume** ⑦.

But it was straight ahead, to the east, through the archway, that Langdon could now see the monolithic Renaissance palace that had become the most famous art museum in the world.

THE SCENE OF THE CRIME: MUSÉE DU LOUVRE ⑧

Langdon felt a familiar tinge of wonder as his eyes made a futile attempt to absorb the entire mass of the edifice. Across a staggeringly expansive plaza, the imposing facade of the Louvre rose like a citadel against the Paris sky. Shaped like an enormous horseshoe, the Louvre was the longest building in Europe, stretching farther than three Eiffel Towers laid end to end. Not even the million square feet of open plaza between the museum wings could challenge the majesty of the facade's breadth. Langdon had once walked the Louvre's entire perimeter, an astonishing three-mile journey.

Despite the estimated five weeks it would take a visitor to properly appreciate the 65,300 pieces of art in this building, most tourists chose an abbreviated experience Langdon referred to as "Louvre Lite"—a full sprint through the museum to see the three most famous objects: the *Mona Lisa*, *Venus de Milo*, and *Winged Victory*. Art Buchwald had once boasted he'd seen all three masterpieces in five minutes and fifty-six seconds.

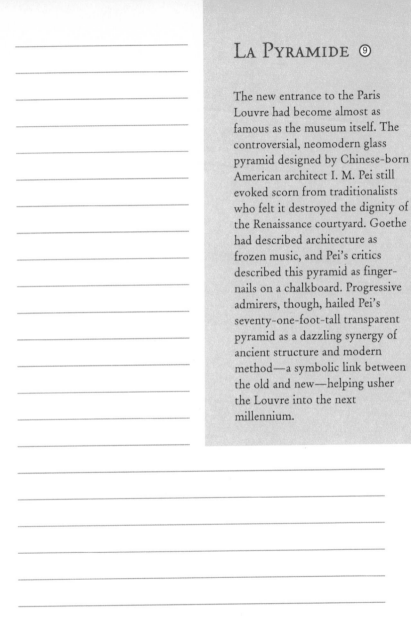

La Pyramide ⑨

The new entrance to the Paris Louvre had become almost as famous as the museum itself. The controversial, neomodern glass pyramid designed by Chinese-born American architect I. M. Pei still evoked scorn from traditionalists who felt it destroyed the dignity of the Renaissance courtyard. Goethe had described architecture as frozen music, and Pei's critics described this pyramid as fingernails on a chalkboard. Progressive admirers, though, hailed Pei's seventy-one-foot-tall transparent pyramid as a dazzling synergy of ancient structure and modern method—a symbolic link between the old and new—helping usher the Louvre into the next millennium.

O, Draconian devil!

Oh, lame saint!

Leonardo da Vinci!
The Mona Lisa!

The *Mona Lisa*'s status as the most famous piece of art in the world, Langdon knew, had nothing to do with her enigmatic smile. Nor was it due to the mysterious interpretations attributed her by many art historians and conspiracy buffs. Quite simply, the *Mona Lisa* was famous because Leonardo da Vinci claimed she was his finest accomplishment. He carried the painting with him whenever he traveled and, if asked why, would reply that he found it hard to part with his most sublime expression of female beauty.

. . .

Standing at an overhead projector in a darkened penitentiary library, Langdon had shared the *Mona Lisa*'s secret with the prisoners attending class, men whom he found surprisingly engaged—rough, but sharp. "You may notice," Langdon told them, walking up to the projected image of the *Mona Lisa* on the library wall, "that the background behind her face is uneven." Langdon motioned to the glaring discrepancy. "Da Vinci painted the horizon line on the left significantly lower than the right."

"He screwed it up?" one of the inmates asked.

Langdon chuckled. "No. Da Vinci didn't do that too often. Actually, this is a little trick Da Vinci played. By lowering the countryside on the left, Da Vinci made Mona Lisa look much larger from the left side than from the right side. A little Da Vinci inside joke. Historically, the concepts of male and female have assigned sides— left is female, and right is male. Because Da Vinci was a big fan of feminine principles, he made Mona Lisa look more majestic from the *left* than the right."

. . .

"Hey, Mr. Langford," a muscle-bound man said. "Is it true that the *Mona Lisa* is a picture of Da Vinci in drag? I heard that was true."

"It's quite possible," Langdon said. "Da Vinci was a prankster, and computerized analysis of the *Mona Lisa* and Da Vinci's self-portraits confirm some startling points of congruency in their faces. Whatever Da Vinci was up to," Langdon said, "his *Mona Lisa* is neither male nor female. It carries a subtle message of androgyny. It is a fusing of both."

"You sure that's not just some Harvard bullshit way of saying Mona Lisa is one ugly chick."

Now Langdon laughed. "You may be right. But actually Da Vinci left a big clue that the painting was supposed to be androgynous. Has anyone here ever heard of an Egyptian god named Amon?"

"Hell yes!" the big guy said. "God of masculine fertility!"

. . .

"And do you know who Amon's counterpart was? The Egyptian *goddess* of fertility?"

The question met with several seconds of silence.

"It was Isis," Langdon told them, grabbing a grease pen. "So we have the male god, Amon." He wrote it down. "And the female goddess, Isis, whose ancient pictogram was once called L'ISA."

Langdon finished writing and stepped back from the projector.

AMON L'ISA

"Ring any bells?" he asked.

"Mona Lisa!" somebody gasped.

Langdon nodded. "Gentlemen, not only does the face of Mona Lisa look androgynous, but her name is an anagram of the divine union of male and female. And *that*, my friends, is Da Vinci's little secret, and the reason for Mona Lisa's knowing smile."

Madonna of the Rocks

Da Vinci's original commission for *Madonna of the Rocks* had come from an organization known as the Confraternity of the Immaculate Conception, which needed a painting for the centerpiece of an altar triptych in their church of San Francesco in Milan. The nuns gave Leonardo specific dimensions, and the desired theme for the painting—the Virgin Mary, baby John the Baptist, Uriel, and Baby Jesus sheltering in a cave. Although Da Vinci did as they requested, when he delivered the work, the group reacted with horror. He had filled the painting with explosive and disturbing details.

The painting showed a blue-robed Virgin Mary sitting with her arm around an infant child, presumably Baby Jesus. Opposite Mary sat Uriel, also with an infant, presumably baby John the Baptist. Oddly, though, rather than the usual Jesus-blessing-John scenario, it was baby *John* who was blessing Jesus . . . and Jesus was submitting to his authority! More troubling still, Mary was holding one hand high above the head of infant John and making a decidedly threatening gesture—her fingers looking like eagle's talons, gripping an invisible head.

Finally, the most obvious and frightening image: Just below Mary's curled fingers, Uriel was making a cutting gesture with his hand—as if slicing the neck of the invisible head gripped by Mary's claw-like hand.

ARC DE TRIOMPHE ⑩

As Sophie accelerated, Langdon sensed she was formulating a plan. Dead ahead, at the end of Champs-Elysées, stood the Arc de Triomphe —Napoleon's 164-foot-tall tribute to his own military potency—encircled by France's largest rotary, a nine-lane behemoth.

. . .

She gave him a quick smile and exited the rotary, heading due north, away from the city center. Barely making two green lights, she reached the third intersection and took a hard right onto Boulevard Malesherbes. They'd left the rich, tree-lined streets of the diplomatic neighborhood and plunged into a darker industrial neighborhood. Sophie took a quick left, and a moment later, Langdon realized where they were.

GARE
SAINT-LAZARE ⑪

Ahead of them, the glass-roofed train
terminal resembled the awkward
offspring of an airplane hangar and a
greenhouse. European train stations
never slept. Even at this hour, a
half-dozen taxis idled near the main
entrance. Vendors manned carts of
sandwiches and mineral water while
grungy kids in backpacks emerged
from the station rubbing their eyes,
looking around as if trying to remember what city they were in now.

. . .

As the taxi pulled away from station,
Sophie took out their newly pur-
chased train tickets and tore them up.

Langdon sighed. *Seventy dollars
well spent.*

It was not until their taxi had settled into a monotonous north-bound hum on Rue de Clichy that Langdon felt they'd actually escaped. Out the window to his right, he could see **Montmartre** and the beautiful dome of **Sacré-Coeur** ⑬. The image was interrupted by the flash of police lights sailing past them in the opposite direction.

Langdon and Sophie ducked down as the sirens faded.

Sophie had told the cab driver simply to head out of the city, and from her firmly set jaw, Langdon sensed she was trying to figure out their next move.

Bois de Boulogne ⑭

*An address! My grandfather wrote down
an address!*

"Where is this?" Langdon asked.

Sophie had no idea. Facing front
again, she leaned forward and excitedly
asked the driver, *"Connaissez-vous la
Rue Haxo?"*

. . .

"Fastest route is through Bois de
Boulogne," the driver told her in
French. "Is that okay?"

Sophie frowned. She could think
of far less scandalous routes, but
tonight she was not going to be picky.
"Oui." *We can shock the visiting American.*

. . .

The heavily forested park known as
the Bois de Boulogne was called many
things, but the Parisian cognoscenti
knew it as "the Garden of Earthly
Delights." The epithet, despite sound-
ing flattering, was quite to the contrary.
Anyone who had seen the lurid Bosch
painting of the same name understood
the jab; the painting, like the forest,
was dark and twisted, a purgatory for
freaks and fetishists. At night, the forest's winding lanes were lined with
hundreds of glistening bodies for hire,
earthly delights to satisfy one's deep-
est unspoken desires—male, female,
and everything in between.

LOCATION OF THE DEPOSITORY BANK OF ZURICH (FICTITIOUS)

Rumors existed that the Priory had vowed someday to bring the Grail back to France to a final resting place, but certainly no historical evidence existed to suggest that this indeed had happened. Even if the Priory had managed to bring the Grail back to France, the address 24 Rue Haxo near a tennis stadium hardly sounded like a noble final resting place.

. . .

Sophie snaked her way toward the stadium. After several passes, they located the intersection of Rue Haxo and turned onto it, driving in the direction of the lower numbers. The road became more industrial, lined with businesses.

We need number twenty-four, Langdon told himself, realizing he was secretly scanning the horizon for the spires of a church. *Don't be ridiculous. A forgotten Templar church in this neighborhood?*

"There it is," Sophie exclaimed, pointing.

Langdon's eyes followed to the structure ahead.

What in the world?

The building was modern. A squat citadel with a giant, neon equal-armed cross emblazoned atop its facade. Beneath the cross were the words:

DEPOSITORY BANK OF ZURICH

SILAS FOLLOWS A FALSE CLUE: THE CHURCH OF SAINT-SULPICE ⑮

The Church of Saint-Sulpice, it is said, has the most eccentric history of any building in Paris. Built over the ruins of an ancient temple to the Egyptian goddess Isis, the church possesses an architectural footprint matching that of Notre Dame to within inches. The sanctuary has played host to the baptisms of the Marquis de Sade and Baudelaire, as well as the marriage of Victor Hugo. The attached seminary has a well-documented history of unorthodoxy and was once the clandestine meeting hall for numerous secret societies.

THE ROSE LINE

On a globe, a Rose Line—also called a meridian or longitude—was any imaginary line drawn from the North Pole to the South Pole. There were, of course, an infinite number of Rose Lines because every point on the globe could have a longitude drawn through it connecting north and south poles. The question for early navigators was *which* of these lines would be called *the* Rose Line—the zero longitude—the line from which all other longitudes on earth would be measured.

Today that line was in Greenwich, England.

But it had not always been.

Long before the establishment of Greenwich as the prime meridian, the zero longitude of the entire world had passed directly through Paris, and through the Church of Saint-Sulpice. The brass marker in Saint-Sulpice was a memorial to the world's first prime meridian, and although Greenwich had stripped Paris of the honor in 1888, the original Rose Line was still visible today.

The Grail Quest Continues with Sir Leigh Teabing

As the armored truck accelerated again, Langdon was pleased how much more smoothly it drove. "Do you know how to get to Versailles?"

Sophie eyed him. "Sightseeing?"

"No, I have a plan. There's a religious historian I know who lives near Versailles. I can't remember exactly where, but we can look it up. I've been to his estate a few times. His name is Leigh Teabing. He's a former British Royal Historian."

. . .

"Let's hope Leigh doesn't mind late-night visitors."

"For the record, it's *Sir* Leigh." Langdon had made that mistake only once. "Teabing is quite a character. He was knighted by the Queen several years back after composing an extensive history on the House of York."

Sophie looked over. "You're kidding, right? We're going to visit a *knight*?"

Langdon gave an awkward smile. "We're on a Grail quest, Sophie. Who better to help us than a knight?"

Château Villette

The sprawling 185-acre estate of
Château Villette was located twenty-
five minutes northwest of Paris in the
environs of Versailles. Designed by
François Mansart in 1668 for the
Count of Aufflay, it was one of Paris's
most significant historical châteaux.
Complete with two rectangular lakes
and gardens designed by Le Nôtre,
Château Villette was more of a modest castle than a mansion. The estate
fondly had become known as *la Petite
Versailles*.

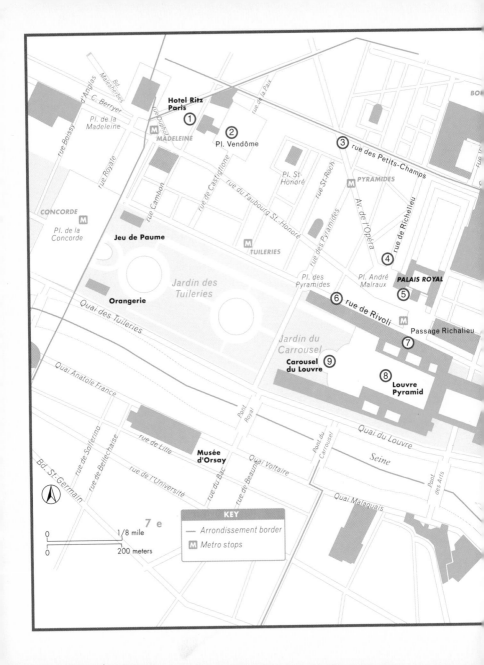

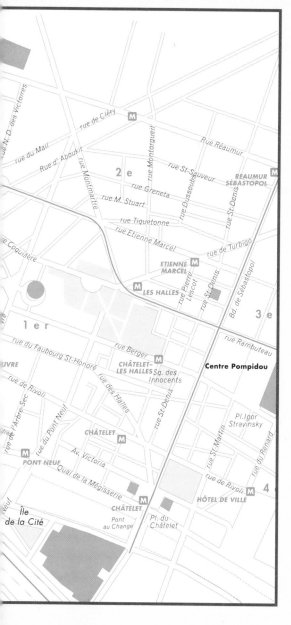

PARIS:
The True Resting Place of the Grail?

① **Hotel Ritz Paris**

② **Place Vendôme**

③ **Rue des Petits Champs**

④ **Rue Richelieu**

⑤ **Palais Royal**

⑥ **Rue de Rivoli**

⑦ **Passage Richelieu**

⑧ **The Louvre Pyramid**

⑨ **Carrousel du Louvre**

Langdon's Epilogue Discovery

Robert Langdon awoke with a start. He had been dreaming. The bathrobe beside his bed bore the monogram **Hotel Ritz Paris ①**. He saw a dim light filtering through the blinds. *Is it dusk or dawn?* he wondered.

. . .

Twenty minutes later, Langdon stepped out of the Hotel Ritz into **Place Vendôme ②**. Night was falling. The days of sleep had left him disoriented . . . and yet his mind felt oddly lucid. He had promised himself he would stop in the hotel lobby for a café au lait to clear his thoughts, but instead his legs carried him directly out the front door into the gathering Paris night.

Walking east on **Rue des Petits Champs ③**, Langdon felt a growing excitement. He turned south onto **Rue Richelieu ④**, where the air grew sweet with the scent of blossoming jasmine from the stately gardens of the **Palais Royal ⑤**.

He continued south until he saw what he was looking for—the famous royal arcade—a glistening expanse of polished black marble. Moving onto it, Langdon scanned the surface beneath his feet. Within seconds, he found what he knew was there—several bronze medallions embedded in the ground in a perfectly straight line. Each disk was five inches in diameter and embossed with the letters N and S.

Nord. Sud.

He turned due south, letting his eye trace the extended line formed by the medallions. He began moving again, following the trail, watching the pavement as he walked. As he cut across the corner of the Comédie-Française, another bronze medallion passed beneath his feet. *Yes!*

The streets of Paris, Langdon had learned years ago, were adorned with 135 of these bronze markers, embedded in sidewalks, courtyards, and streets, on a north-south axis across the city. He had once followed the line from Sacré-Coeur, south across the Seine, and finally to the ancient Paris Observatory. There he discovered the significance of the sacred path it traced.

The earth's original prime meridian.

The first zero longitude of the world.

Paris's ancient Rose Line.

Now, as Langdon hurried across **Rue de Rivoli ⑥**, he could feel his destination within reach. Less than a block away.

THE HOLY GRAIL 'NEATH ANCIENT

ROSLIN WAITS.

· · ·

He broke into a jog, feeling the Rose Line beneath his feet, guiding him, pulling him toward his destination. As he entered the long tunnel of **Passage Richelieu ⑦**, the hairs on his neck began to bristle with anticipation. He knew that at the end of this tunnel stood the most mysterious of Parisian monuments—conceived and commissioned in the 1980s by the Sphinx himself, François Mitterrand, a man rumored to move in secret circles, a man whose final legacy to Paris was a place Langdon had visited only days before.

. . .

The Louvre Pyramid ⑧.

Gleaming in the darkness.

He admired it only a moment. He was more interested in what lay to his right. Turning, he felt his feet again tracing the invisible path of the ancient Rose Line, carrying him across the courtyard to the **Carrousel du Louvre ⑨**—the enormous circle of grass surrounded by a perimeter of neatly trimmed hedges—once the site of Paris's primeval nature-worshipping festivals . . . joyous rites to celebrate fertility and the Goddess.

Langdon felt as if he were crossing into another world as he stepped over the bushes to the grassy area within. This hallowed ground was now marked by one of the city's most unusual monuments. There in the center, plunging into the earth like a crystal chasm, gaped the giant inverted pyramid of glass that he had seen a few nights ago when he entered the Louvre's subterranean entresol.

La Pyramide Inversée.

. . .

Langdon felt himself awaken fully now to the thrill of unthinkable possibility. Raising his eyes again to the Louvre, he sensed the huge wings of the museum enveloping him . . . hallways that burgeoned with the world's finest art.

Da Vinci . . . Botticelli . . .

ADORNED IN MASTERS' LOVING ART,
SHE LIES.

. . .

Stepping out of the circle, he hurried across the courtyard back toward the towering pyramid entrance of the Louvre. The day's last visitors were trickling out of the museum.

Pushing through the revolving door, Langdon descended the curved staircase into the pyramid. He could feel the air grow cooler. When he reached the bottom, he entered the long tunnel that stretched beneath the Louvre's courtyard, back toward *La Pyramide Inversée*.

At the end of the tunnel, he emerged into a large chamber. Directly before him, hanging down from above, gleamed the inverted pyramid—a breathtaking V-shaped contour of glass.

The Chalice.

Langdon's eyes traced its narrowing form downward to its tip, suspended only six feet above the floor. There, directly beneath it, stood the tiny structure.

A miniature pyramid. Only three feet tall. The only structure in this colossal complex that had been built on a small scale.

. . .

Illuminated in the soft lights of the deserted entresol, the two pyramids pointed at one another, their bodies perfectly aligned, their tips almost touching.

The Chalice above. The Blade below.

THE BLADE AND CHALICE
GUARDING O'ER HER GATES.

Langdon heard Marie Chauvel's words. *One day it will dawn on you.*

He was standing beneath the ancient Rose Line, surrounded by the work of masters. What better place for Saunière to keep watch? Now at last, he sensed he understood the true meaning of the Grand Master's verse. Raising his eyes to heaven, he gazed upward through the glass to a glorious, star-filled night.

SHE RESTS AT LAST BENEATH THE
STARRY SKIES.

LONDON

"You'll be pleased to hear that at least we're flying in the right direction."

Langdon examined the thick vellum sheet. Written in ornate penmanship was another four-line verse. Again, in iambic pentameter. The verse was cryptic, but Langdon needed to read only as far as the first line to realize that Teabing's plan to come to Britain was going to pay off.

IN LONDON LIES A KNIGHT A POPE INTERRED.

The remainder of the poem clearly implied that the password for opening the second cryptex could be found by visiting this knight's tomb, somewhere in the city.

Langdon turned excitedly to Teabing. "Do you have any idea what knight this poem is referring to?"

Teabing grinned. "Not the foggiest. But I know in precisely which crypt we should look."

LONDON

"You'll be pleased to hear that at least we're flying in the right direction."

Langdon examined the thick vellum sheet. Written in ornate penmanship was another four-line verse. Again, in iambic pentameter. The verse was cryptic, but Langdon needed to read only as far as the first line to realize that Teabing's plan to come to Britain was going to pay off.

IN LONDON LIES A KNIGHT A POPE INTERRED.

The remainder of the poem clearly implied that the password for opening the second cryptex could be found by visiting this knight's tomb, somewhere in the city.

Langdon turned excitedly to Teabing. "Do you have any idea what knight this poem is referring to?"

Teabing grinned. "Not the foggiest. But I know in precisely which crypt we should look."

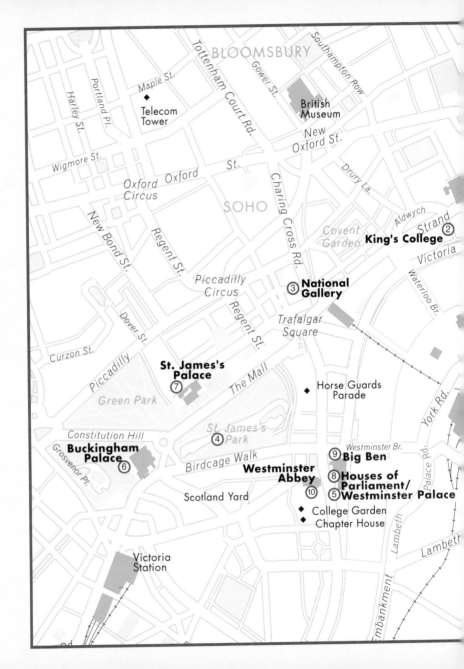

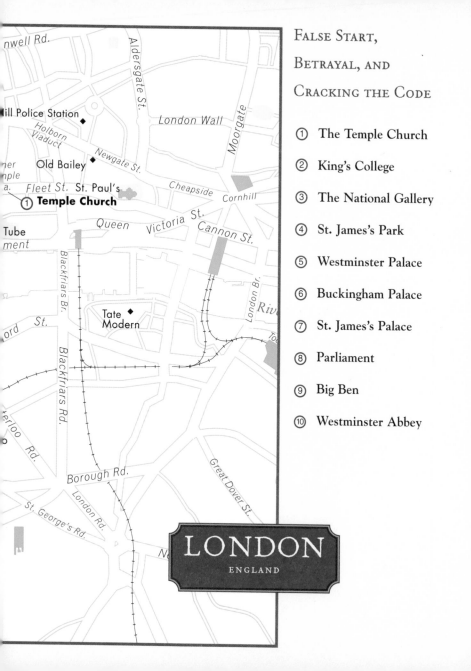

FALSE START,
BETRAYAL, AND
CRACKING THE CODE

① The Temple Church

② King's College

③ The National Gallery

④ St. James's Park

⑤ Westminster Palace

⑥ Buckingham Palace

⑦ St. James's Palace

⑧ Parliament

⑨ Big Ben

⑩ Westminster Abbey

LONDON
ENGLAND

THE TEMPLE CHURCH ①

"Fleet Street?" Langdon asked, eyeing Teabing in the back of the limo. There's a crypt on Fleet Street? So far, Leigh was being playfully cagey about where he thought they would find the "knight's tomb," which, according to the poem, would provide the password for opening the smaller cryptex.

Teabing grinned and turned to Sophie. "Miss Neveu, give the Harvard boy one more shot at the verse, will you?"

. . .

In London lies a knight a Pope
    interred.
His labor's fruit a Holy wrath
    incurred.
You seek the orb that ought be on his
    tomb.
It speaks of Rosy flesh and seeded
    womb.

. . .

Langdon thought of the notorious Templar round-up in 1307—unlucky Friday the thirteenth—when Pope Clement killed and interred hundreds of Knights Templar. "But there must be endless graves of 'knights killed by Popes.' "

"Aha, not so!" Teabing said. "Many of them were burned at the stake and tossed unceremoniously into the Tiber River. But this poem refers to a tomb. A tomb in London. And there are few knights buried in London." He paused, eyeing Langdon as if waiting for light to dawn. Finally he huffed. "Robert, for heaven's sake! The church built in London by the Priory's military arm—the Knights Templar themselves!"

"The Temple Church?" Langdon drew a startled breath. "It has a crypt?"

"Ten of the most frightening tombs you will ever see."

Langdon had never actually visited the Temple Church, although he'd come across numerous references in his Priory research. Once the epicenter of all Templar/Priory activities in the United Kingdom, the Temple Church had been so named in honor of Solomon's Temple, from which the Knights Templar had extracted their own title, as well as the Sangreal documents that gave them all their influence in Rome. Tales abounded of knights performing strange, secretive rituals within the Temple Church's unusual sanctuary. "The Temple Church is on Fleet Street?"

. . .

CONTINUED . . .

"The church is hidden now behind much larger buildings. Few people even know it's there. Eerie old place. The architecture is pagan to the core."

Sophie looked surprised. "Pagan?"

"Pantheonically pagan!" Teabing exclaimed. "The church is *round*. The Templars ignored the traditional Christian cruciform layout and built a perfectly circular church in honor of the sun." His eyebrows did a devilish dance. "A not so subtle howdy-do to the boys in Rome. They might as well have resurrected Stonehenge in downtown London."

. . .

London's ancient Temple Church was constructed entirely of Caen stone. A dramatic, circular edifice with a daunting facade, a central turret, and a protruding nave off one side, the church looked more like a military stronghold than a place of worship. Consecrated on the tenth of February in 1185 by Heraclius, Patriarch of Jerusalem, the Temple Church survived eight centuries of political turmoil, the Great Fire of London, and the First World War, only to be heavily damaged by Luftwaffe incendiary bombs in 1940. After the war, it was restored to its original, stark grandeur.

CONTINUED . . .

The simplicity of the circle, Langdon thought, admiring the building for the first time. The architecture was coarse and simple, more reminiscent of Rome's rugged Castel Sant'Angelo than the refined Pantheon. The boxy annex jutting out to the right was an unfortunate eyesore, although it did little to shroud the original pagan shape of the primary structure.

. . .

As they arrived outside the circular chamber, Teabing shot a glance over his shoulder at the altar boy, who was vacuuming in the distance. "You know," Teabing whispered to Sophie, "the Holy Grail is said to once have been stored in this church overnight while the Templars moved it from one hiding place to another. Can you

CONTINUED . . .

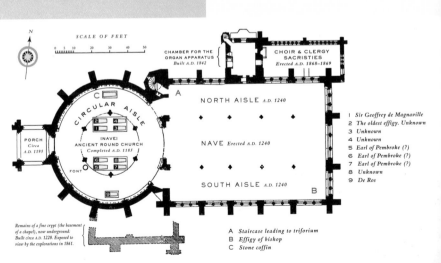

N

SCALE OF FEET

0 5 10 20 30 40 50

CHAMBER FOR THE
ORGAN APPARATUS
Built A.D. 1842

CHOIR & CLERGY
SACRISTIES
Erected A.D. 1868–1869

A

NORTH AISLE A.D. 1240

C

CIRCULAR AISLE

2 4
1 3

NAVE *Erected A.D. 1240*

PORCH
*Circa
A.D. 1195*

NAVE
ANCIENT ROUND CHURCH
Completed A.D. 1185

6 5
7 8

FONT

9

SOUTH AISLE A.D. 1240

B

1 *Sir Geoffrey de Magnaville*
2 *The oldest effigy. Unknown*
3 *Unknown*
4 *Unknown*
5 *Earl of Pembroke (?)*
6 *Earl of Pembroke (?)*
7 *Earl of Pembroke (?)*
8 *Unknown*
9 *De Ros*

*Remains of a fine crypt (the basement
of a chapel), now underground:
Built circa A.D. 1220. Exposed to
view by the explorations in 1861.*

A *Staircase leading to triforium*
B *Effigy of bishop*
C *Stone coffin*

imagine the four chests of Sangreal documents sitting right here with Mary Magdalene's sarcophagus? It gives me gooseflesh."

Langdon was feeling gooseflesh too as they stepped into the circular chamber. His eye traced the curvature of the chamber's pale stone perimeter, taking in the carvings of gargoyles, demons, monsters, and pained human faces, all staring inward. Beneath the carvings, a single stone pew curled around the entire circumference of the room.

"Theater in the round," Langdon whispered.

Teabing raised a crutch, pointing toward the far left of the room and then to the far right. Langdon had already seen them.

Ten stone knights.
Five on the left. Five on the right.

Lying supine on the floor, the carved, life-sized figures rested in peaceful poses. The knights were depicted wearing full armor, shields, and swords, and the tombs gave Langdon the uneasy sensation that someone had snuck in and poured plaster over the knights while they were sleeping. All of the figures were deeply weathered, and yet each was clearly unique— different armory pieces, distinct leg and arm positions, facial features, and markings on their shields.

In London lies a knight a Pope interred.

Langdon felt shaky as he inched deeper into the circular room.

This had to be the place.

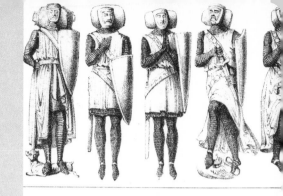

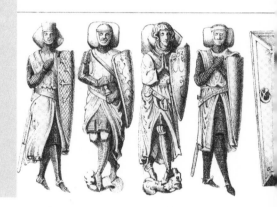

King's College ②

King's College, established by King George IV in 1829, houses its Department of Theology and Religious Studies adjacent to Parliament on property granted by the Crown. King's College Religion Department boasts not only 150 years' experience in teaching and research, but the 1982 establishment of the Research Institute in Systematic Theology, which possesses one of the most complete and electronically advanced religious research libraries in the world.

Langdon still felt shaky as he and Sophie came in from the rain and entered the library. The primary research room was as Teabing had described it—a dramatic octagonal chamber dominated by an enormous round table around which King Arthur and his knights might have been comfortable were it not for the presence of twelve flat-screen computer workstations.

In London lies a knight a Pope interred.
His labor's fruit a Holy wrath incurred.
You seek the orb that ought be on his tomb.
It speaks of Rosy flesh and seeded womb.

Virgin of the Rocks, The National Gallery ③

Langdon's students were always amused to learn that Da Vinci eventually mollified the confraternity by painting a second, "watered-down" version of *Madonna of the Rocks* in which everyone was arranged in a more orthodox manner. The second version now hung in London's National Gallery under the name *Virgin of the Rocks*, although Langdon still preferred the Louvre's more intriguing original.

St. James's Park ④

St. James's Park is a sea of green in the
middle of London, a public park
bordering the palaces of **Westminster**
⑤, **Buckingham** ⑥, and **St. James's** ⑦.
Once enclosed by King Henry VIII
and stocked with deer for the hunt,
St. James's Park is now open to the
public. On sunny afternoons,
Londoners picnic beneath the willows
and feed the pond's resident pelicans,
whose ancestors were a gift to Charles
II from the Russian ambassador.

The Teacher saw no pelicans
today. The stormy weather had
brought instead seagulls from the
ocean. The lawns were covered with
them—hundreds of white bodies all
facing the same direction, patiently
riding out the damp wind. Despite
the morning fog, the park afforded
splendid views of the Houses of
Parliament ⑧ and **Big Ben** ⑨. Gazing
across the sloping lawns, past the
duck pond and the delicate silhouettes
of the weeping willows, the Teacher
could see the spires of the building
that housed the knight's tomb—the
real reason he had told Rémy to come
to this spot.

your photo of Big Ben
here

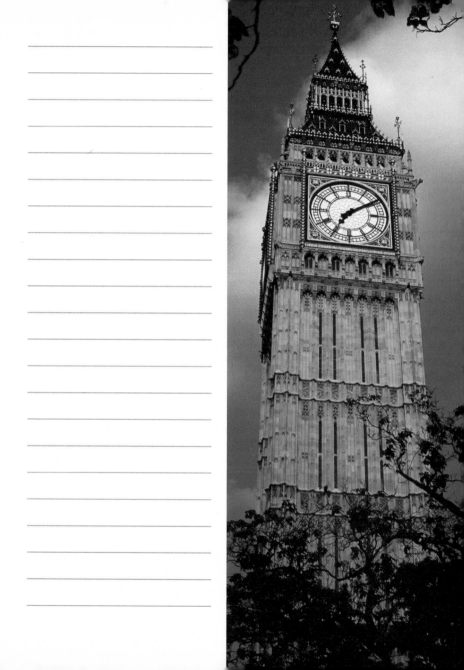

WESTMINSTER ABBEY ⑩

More than three thousand people are entombed or enshrined within Westminster Abbey. The colossal stone interior burgeons with the remains of kings, statesmen, scientists, poets, and musicians. Their tombs, packed into every last niche and alcove, range in grandeur from the most regal of mausoleums— that of Queen Elizabeth I, whose canopied sarcophagus inhabits its own private, apsidal chapel—down to the most modest etched floor tiles whose inscriptions have worn away with centuries of foot traffic, leaving it to one's imagination whose relics might lie below the tile in the undercroft.

Designed in the style of the great cathedrals of Amiens, Chartres, and Canterbury, Westminster Abbey is considered neither cathedral nor parish church. It bears the classification of *royal peculiar*, subject only to the Sovereign. Since hosting the coronation of William the Conqueror on Christmas Day in 1066, the dazzling sanctuary has witnessed an endless procession of royal ceremonies and affairs of state—from the canonization of Edward the Confessor, to the marriage of Prince Andrew and Sarah Ferguson, to the funerals of Henry V, Queen Elizabeth I, and Diana, Princess of Wales.

. . .

"Which way is it?" Sophie asked, looking around.

The tomb. Langdon had no idea. "We should find a docent and ask."

Langdon knew better than to wander aimlessly in here. Westminster Abbey was a tangled warren of mausoleums, perimeter chambers, and walk-in burial niches. Like the Louvre's Grand Gallery, it had a lone point of entry—the door through which they had just passed—easy to find your way in, but impossible to find your way out. A literal tourist trap, one of Langdon's befuddled colleagues had called it. Keeping architectural tradition, the abbey was laid out in the shape of a giant crucifix. Unlike most churches, however, it had its entrance on the side, rather than the standard rear of the church via the narthex at the bottom of the nave. Moreover, the abbey had a series of sprawling cloisters attached. One false step through the wrong archway, and a visitor was lost in a labyrinth of outdoor passageways surrounded by high walls.

Newton's Tomb, Westminster Abbey

 Newton's tomb consisted of a massive black-marble sarcophagus on which reclined the sculpted form of Sir Isaac Newton, wearing classical costume, and leaning proudly against a stack of his own books—*Divinity, Chronology, Opticks,* and *Philosophiae Naturalis Principia Mathematica.* At Newton's feet stood two winged boys holding a scroll. Behind Newton's recumbent body rose an austere pyramid. Although the pyramid itself seemed an oddity, it was the giant shape mounted halfway up the pyramid that most intrigued the Teacher.

An orb.

The Teacher pondered Saunière's beguiling riddle. *You seek the orb that ought be on his tomb.* The massive orb protruding from the face of the pyramid was carved in basso-relievo and depicted all kinds of heavenly bodies—constellations, signs of the zodiac, comets, stars, and planets. Above it, the image of the Goddess of Astronomy beneath a field of stars.

Countless orbs.

. . .

What orb ought to be here . . . and yet is missing?

THE
CHAPTER HOUSE,
WESTMINSTER ABBEY

I have Teabing.
Go through
Chapter House,
out south exit,
to public garden
. . .

As they hurried down the dark corridor, the sounds of the wind and rain from the open cloister faded behind them. The Chapter House was a kind of satellite structure—a freestanding annex at the end of the long hallway to ensure the privacy of the Parliament proceedings housed there.

"It looks huge," Sophie whispered as they approached.

Langdon had forgotten just how large this room was. Even from outside the entrance, he could gaze across the vast expanse of floor to the breathtaking windows on the far side of the octagon, which rose five stories to a vaulted ceiling. They would certainly have a clear view of the garden from in here.

Crossing the threshold, both Langdon and Sophie found themselves having to squint. After the gloomy cloisters, the Chapter House felt like a solarium. They were a good ten feet into the room, searching the south wall, when they realized the door they had been promised was not there.

They were standing in an enormous dead end.

The creaking of a heavy door behind them made them turn, just as the door closed with a resounding thud and the latch fell into place. The lone man who had been standing behind the door looked calm as he aimed a small revolver at them. He was portly and was propped on a pair of aluminum crutches.

For a moment Langdon thought he must be dreaming.

It was Leigh Teabing.

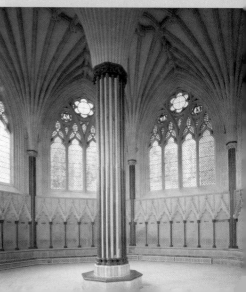

APPLE

"The orb from which Eve partook," Langdon said coolly, "incurring the Holy wrath of God. Original sin. The symbol of the fall of the sacred feminine."

Teabing felt the truth come crashing down on him in excruciating austerity. The orb that ought be on Newton's tomb could be none other than the Rosy apple that fell from heaven, struck Newton on the head, and inspired his life's work. *His labor's fruit! The Rosy flesh with a seeded womb!*

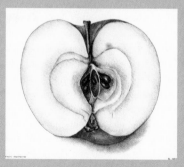

EDINBURGH

The Holy Grail 'neath ancient
Roslin waits.

True Grail academics agreed that Rosslyn was a decoy—
one of the devious dead ends the Priory crafted so convincingly. Tonight, however, with the Priory's keystone
offering a verse that pointed directly to this spot,
Langdon no longer felt so smug. A perplexing question
had been running through his mind all day:

*Why would Saunière go to such effort to guide us to so
obvious a location?*

There seemed only one logical answer.

*There is something about Rosslyn we have yet to under-
stand.*

The Holy Grail 'neath ancient
Roslin waits.

True Grail academics agreed that Rosslyn was a decoy—one of the devious dead ends the Priory crafted so convincingly. Tonight, however, with the Priory's keystone offering a verse that pointed directly to this spot, Langdon no longer felt so smug. A perplexing question had been running through his mind all day:

Why would Saunière go to such effort to guide us to so obvious a location?

There seemed only one logical answer.

There is something about Rosslyn we have yet to understand.

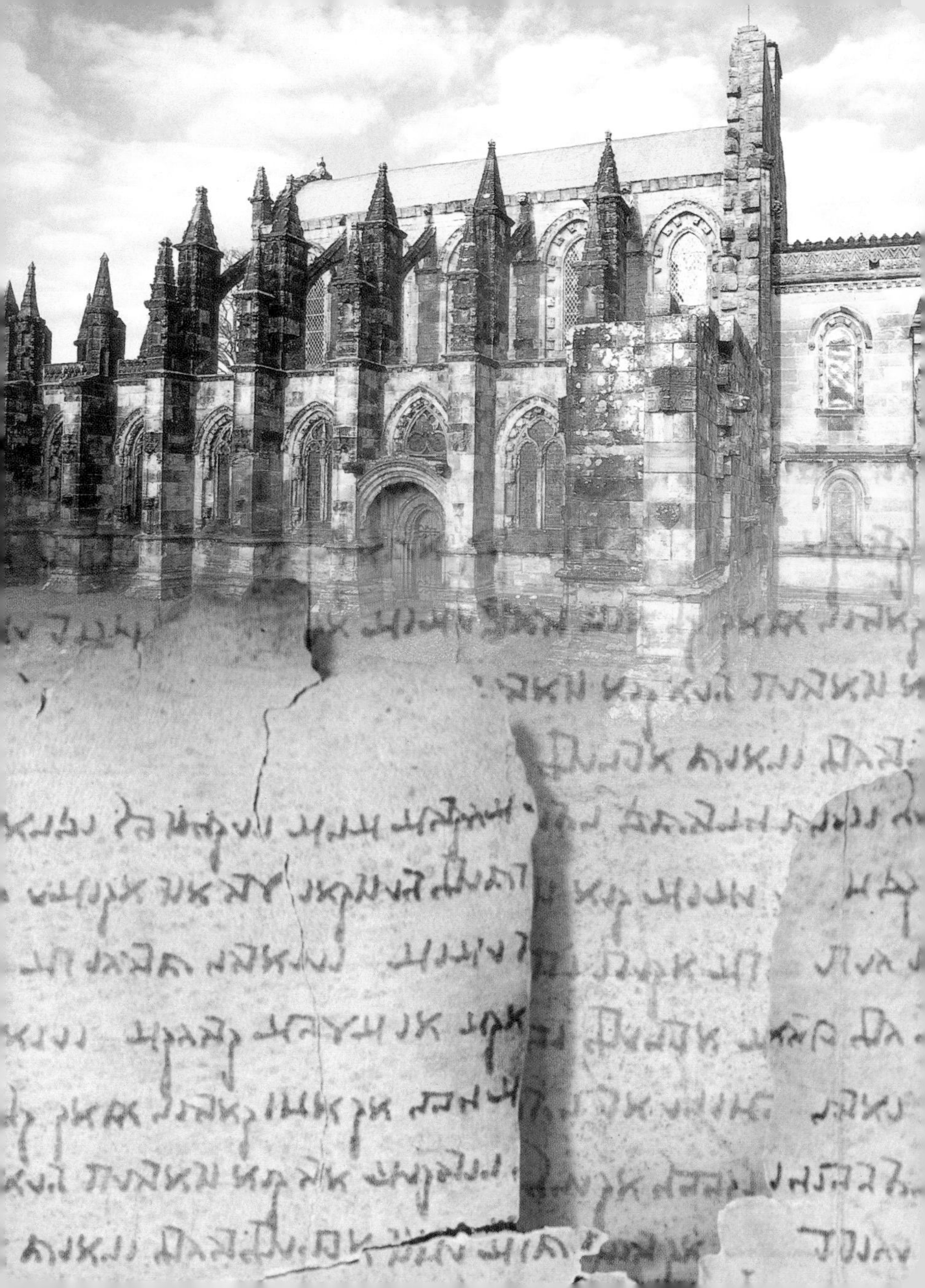

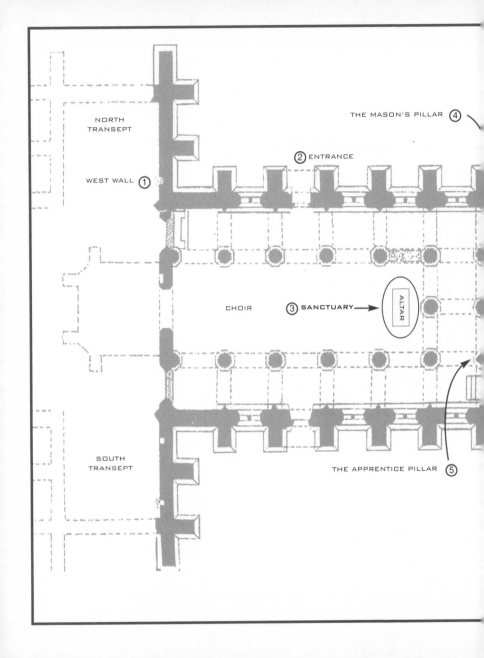

NORTH
TRANSEPT

THE MASON'S PILLAR ④

② ENTRANCE

WEST WALL ①

CHOIR

③ SANCTUARY ⟶ ALTAR

SOUTH
TRANSEPT

THE APPRENTICE PILLAR ⑤

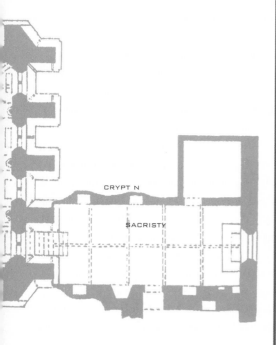

CRYPT N

SACRISTY

ROSSLYN
CHAPEL

The Cathedral
of Codes

ROSSLYN CHAPEL

Rosslyn Chapel—often called the Cathedral of Codes—stands seven miles south of Edinburgh, Scotland, on the site of an ancient Mithraic temple. Built by the Knights Templar in 1446, the chapel is engraved with a mind-boggling array of symbols from the Jewish, Christian, Egyptian, Masonic, and pagan traditions.

The chapel's geographic coordinates fall precisely on the north-south meridian that runs through Glastonbury. This longitudinal Rose Line is the traditional marker of King Arthur's Isle of Avalon and is considered the central pillar of Britain's sacred geometry. It is from this hallowed Rose Line that Rosslyn—originally spelled Roslin—takes its name.

. . .

Langdon had fantasized that Saunière's "Grail map" would be a diagram—a drawing with an X-marks-the-spot—and yet the Priory's final secret had been unveiled in the same way Saunière had spoken to them from the beginning. *Simple verse.* Four explicit lines that pointed without a doubt to this very spot. In addition to identifying Rosslyn by name, the verse made reference to several of the chapel's renowned architectural features.

CONTINUED . . .

Despite the clarity of Saunière's final revelation, Langdon had been left feeling more off balance than enlightened. To him, Rosslyn Chapel seemed far too obvious a location. For centuries, this stone chapel had echoed with whispers of the Holy Grail's presence. The whispers had turned to shouts in recent decades when ground-penetrating radar revealed the presence of an astonishing structure beneath the chapel—a massive subterranean chamber. Not only did this deep vault dwarf the chapel atop it, but it appeared to have no entrance or exit. Archaeologists petitioned to begin blasting through the bedrock to reach the mysterious chamber, but the Rosslyn Trust expressly forbade any excavation of the sacred site. Of course, this only fueled the fires of speculation. What was the Rosslyn Trust trying to hide?

Rosslyn had now become a pilgrimage site for mystery seekers. Some claimed they were drawn here by the powerful magnetic field that emanated inexplicably from these coordinates, some claimed they came to search the hillside for a hidden entrance to the vault, but most admitted they had come simply to wander the grounds and absorb the lore of the Holy Grail.

Langdon and Neveu Explore Rosslyn Chapel

Making their way up the long gravel path, Langdon and Sophie passed the famous **west wall** ① of the chapel. Casual visitors assumed this oddly protruding wall was a section of the chapel that had not been finished. The truth, Langdon recalled, was far more intriguing.

The west wall of Solomon's Temple.

The Knights Templar had designed Rosslyn Chapel as an exact architectural blueprint of Solomon's Temple in Jerusalem—complete with a west wall, a narrow rectangular sanctuary, and a subterranean vault like the Holy of Holies, in which the original nine knights had first unearthed their priceless treasure. Langdon had to admit, there existed an intriguing symmetry in the idea of

_____

_____

_____

_____

_____

the Templars building a modern Grail repository that echoed the Grail's original hiding place.

Rosslyn Chapel's **entrance** ② was more modest than Langdon expected. The small wooden door had two iron hinges and a simple, oak sign.

ROSLIN

This ancient spelling, Langdon explained to Sophie, derived from the Rose Line meridian on which the chapel sat; or, as Grail academics preferred to believe, from the "Line of Rose"—the ancestral lineage of Mary Magdalene.

The chapel would be closing soon, and as Langdon pulled open the door, a warm puff of air escaped, as if the ancient edifice were heaving a weary sigh at the end of a long day. Her entry arches burgeoned with carved cinquefoils.

Roses. The womb of the goddess.

CONTINUED . . .

Entering with Sophie, Langdon felt his eyes reaching across the famous **sanctuary** ③ and taking it all in. Although he had read accounts of Rosslyn's arrestingly intricate stonework, seeing it in person was an overwhelming encounter.

Symbology heaven, one of Langdon's colleagues had called it.

Every surface in the chapel had been carved with symbols—Christian cruciforms, Jewish stars, Masonic seals, Templar crosses, cornucopias, pyramids, astrological signs, plants, vegetables, pentacles, and roses. The Knights Templar had been master stonemasons, erecting Templar churches all over Europe, but Rosslyn was considered their most sublime labor of love and veneration. The master masons had left no stone uncarved. Rosslyn Chapel was a shrine to all faiths . . . to all traditions . . . and, above all, to nature and the goddess.

. . .

Langdon looked at the pair of intricately sculpted columns at the far end of the sanctuary. Their white lacework carvings seemed to smolder with a ruddy flow as the last of the day's sunlight streamed in through the west window. The pillars—positioned where the altar would

CONTINUED . . .

normally stand—were an oddly matched pair. The pillar on the left was carved with simple, vertical lines, while the pillar on the right was embellished with an ornate, flowering spiral.

Sophie was already moving toward them. Langdon hurried after her, and as they reached the pillars, Sophie was nodding with incredulity. "Yes, I'm positive I have seen these!"

"I don't doubt you've seen them," Langdon said, "but it wasn't necessarily *here*."

She turned. "What do you mean?"

"These two pillars are the most duplicated architectural structures in history. Replicas exist all over the world."

"Replicas of Rosslyn?" She looked skeptical.

"No. Of the pillars. Do you remember earlier that I mentioned Rosslyn *itself* is a copy of Solomon's Temple? Those two pillars are exact replicas of the two pillars that stood at the head of Solomon's Temple." Langdon pointed to the pillar on the left. "That's called *Boaz*—or the **Mason's Pillar** ④. The other is called *Jachin*—or the **Apprentice Pillar** ⑤." He paused. "In fact, virtually every Masonic temple in the world has two pillars like these."

. . .

CONTINUED . . .

"The code," Sophie blurted, in sudden revelation. "There's a code here!"

The docent looked pleased by her enthusiasm. "Yes there is, ma'am."

"It's on the ceiling," she said, turning to the right-hand wall. "Somewhere over . . . there."

He smiled. "Not your first visit to Rosslyn, I see."

The code, Langdon thought. He had forgotten that little bit of lore. Among Rosslyn's numerous mysteries was a vaulted archway from which hundreds of stone blocks protruded, jutting down to form a bizarre multi-faceted surface. Each block was carved with a symbol, seemingly at random, creating a cipher of unfathomable proportion. Some people believed the code revealed the entrance to the vault beneath the chapel. Others believed it told the true Grail legend. Not that it mattered—cryptographers had been trying for centuries to decipher its meaning. To this day the Rosslyn Trust offered a generous reward to anyone who could unveil the secret meaning, but the code remained a mystery.

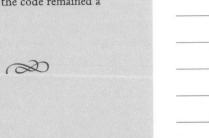

Five-Petal Rose

Rosa rugosa, one of the oldest species of rose, had five petals and pentagonal symmetry, just like the guiding star of Venus, giving the Rose strong iconographic ties to *woman-hood*. In addition, the Rose had close ties to the concept of "true direction" and navigating one's way. The Compass Rose helped travelers navigate, as did Rose Lines, the longitudinal lines on maps. For this reason, the Rose was a symbol that spoke of the Grail on many levels—secrecy, womanhood, and guidance—the feminine chalice and guiding star that led to secret truth.

SUBPLOTS
AND
SIDETRIPS

The Papal Summer Residence, Castel Gandolfo

Vatican Astronomy Library, Castel Gandolfo

Galleria Dell'Accademia, Venice

Santa Maria Dell Grazie, Milan

The Opus Dei National Headquarters, New York

The Papal Summer Residence, Castel Gandolfo

Vatican Astronomy Library, Castel Gandolfo

Galleria Dell'Accademia, Venice

Santa Maria Dell Grazie, Milan

The Opus Dei National Headquarters, New York

THE PAPAL SUMMER RESIDENCE, CASTEL GANDOLFO

On that night, months ago, as the Fiat had left the airport, Aringarosa was surprised to find himself heading not toward Vatican City but rather eastward up a sinuous mountain road. "Where are we going?" he had demanded of his driver.

"Alban Hills," the man replied. "Your meeting is at Castel Gandolfo."

The Pope's summer residence? Aringarosa had never been, nor had he ever desired to see it. In addition to being the Pope's summer vacation home, the sixteenth-century citadel housed the Specula Vaticana—the

Vatican Observatory—one of the most advanced astronomical observatories in Europe. Aringarosa had never been comfortable with the Vatican's historical need to dabble in science. What was the rationale for fusing science and faith? Unbiased science could not possibly be performed by a man who possessed faith in God. Nor did faith have any need for physical confirmation of its beliefs.

Nonetheless, there it is, he thought as Castel Gandolfo came into view, rising against a star-filled November sky. From the access road, Gandolfo resembled a great stone monster pondering a suicidal leap. Perched at the very edge of a cliff, the castle leaned out over the cradle of Italian civilization—the valley where the Curiazi and Orazi clans fought long before the founding of Rome.

VATICAN ASTRONOMY LIBRARY, CASTEL GANDOLFO

Even in silhouette, Gandolfo was a sight to behold—an impressive example of tiered, defensive architecture, echoing the potency of this dramatic cliffside setting. Sadly, Aringarosa now saw, the Vatican had ruined the building by constructing two huge aluminum telescope domes atop the roof, leaving this once dignified edifice looking like a proud warrior wearing a couple of party hats.

. . .

BIBLIOTECA ASTRONOMICA

Aringarosa had heard of this place— the Vatican's Astronomy Library— rumored to contain more than twenty-five thousand volumes, including rare works of Copernicus, Galileo, Kepler, Newton, and Secchi. Allegedly, it was also the place in which the Pope's highest officers held private meetings . . . those meetings they preferred not to hold within the walls of Vatican City.

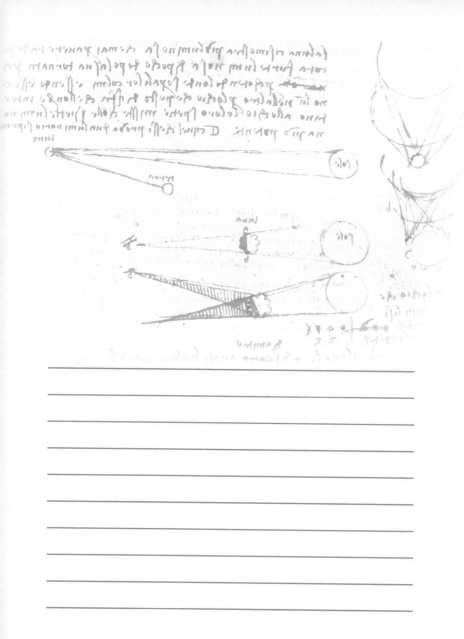

THE PENTACLE

"The pentacle," Langdon clarified, "is a pre-Christian symbol that relates to Nature worship. The ancients envisioned their world in two halves—masculine and feminine. Their gods and goddesses worked to keep a balance of power. Yin and yang. When male and female were balanced, there was harmony in the world. When they were unbalanced, there was chaos."

. . .

"In its most specific interpretation, the pentacle symbolizes Venus—the goddess of female sexual love and beauty."

. . .

"Early religion was based on the divine order of Nature. The goddess

Venus and the planet Venus were one and the same. The goddess had a place in the nighttime sky and was known by many names—Venus, the Eastern Star, Ishtar, Astarte—all of them powerful female concepts with ties to Nature and Mother Earth."

. . .

Langdon decided not to share the pentacle's most astonishing property—the graphic origin of its ties to Venus. As a young astronomy student, Langdon had been stunned to learn the planet Venus traced a perfect pentacle across the ecliptic sky every eight years. So astonished were the ancients to observe this phenomenon, that Venus and her pentacle became symbols of perfection, beauty, and the cyclic qualities of sexual love.

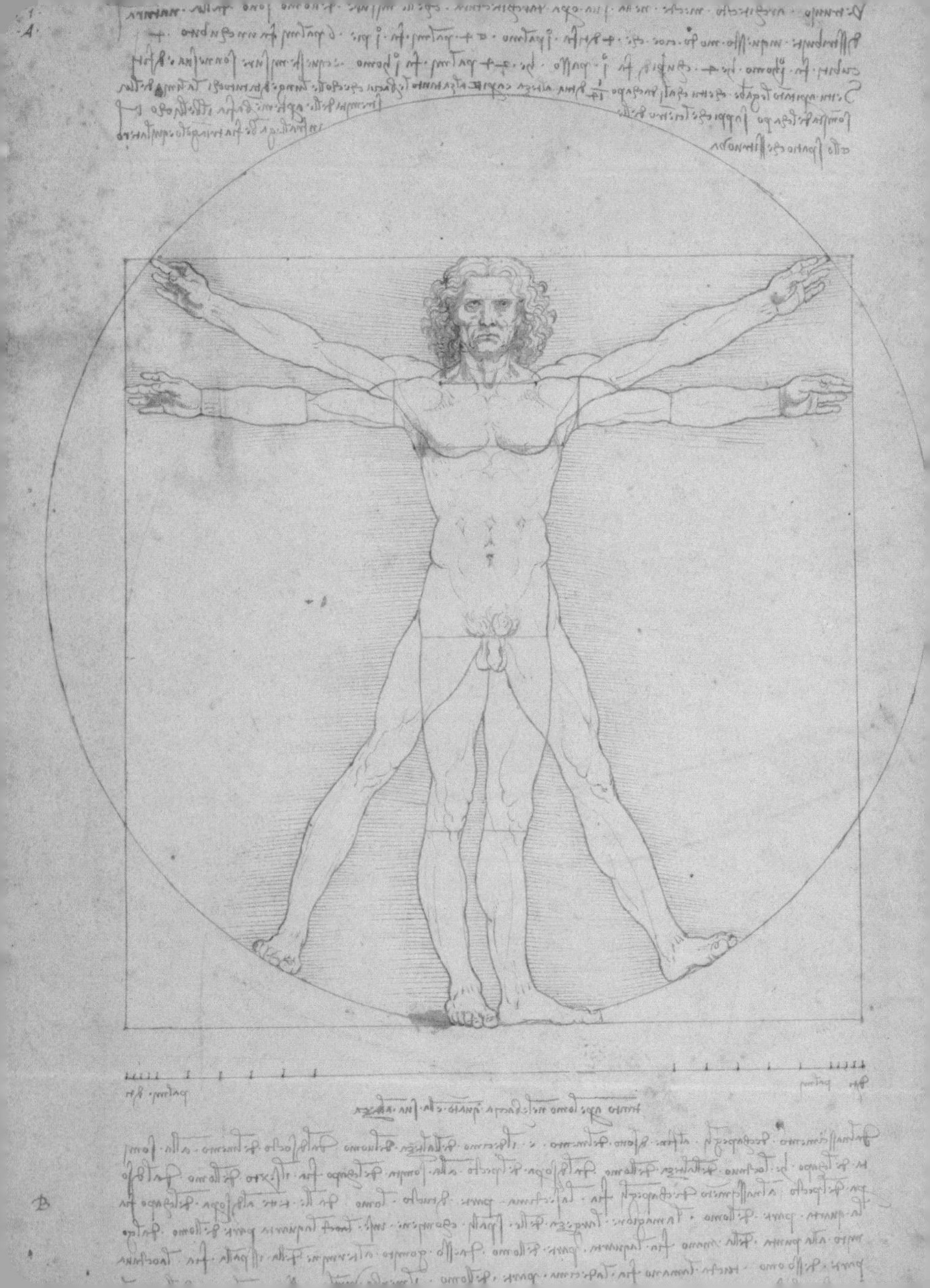

GALLERIA DELL'ACCADEMIA, VENICE

Langdon's Lecture on Divine Proportion and the Vitruvian Man

Da Vinci . . . Fibonacci numbers . . . the pentacle.

Incredibly, all of these things were connected by a single concept so fundamental to art history that Langdon often spent several class periods on the topic.

PHI.

He felt himself suddenly reeling back to Harvard, standing in front of his "Symbolism in Art" class, writing his favorite number on the chalkboard.

1.618

. . .

"This number PHI," Langdon continued, "one-point-six-one-eight, is a very important number in art.

. . .

As Langdon loaded his slide projector, he explained that the number PHI was derived from the Fibonacci sequence—a progression famous not only because the sum of adjacent terms equaled the next term, but because the *quotients* of adjacent terms possessed the astonishing property of approaching the number 1.618—PHI!

Despite PHI's seemingly mystical mathematical origins, Langdon explained, the truly mind-boggling aspect of PHI was its role as a fundamental building block in nature. Plants, animals, and even human beings all possessed dimensional properties that adhered with eerie exactitude to the ratio of PHI to 1.

"PHI's ubiquity in nature," Langdon said, killing the lights, "clearly exceeds coincidence, and so the ancients assumed the number PHI must have been preordained by the Creator of the universe. Early scientists heralded one-point-six-one-eight as the Divine *Proportion*."

. . .

He pulled up another slide—a pale yellow parchment displaying Leonardo da Vinci's famous male nude—*The Vitruvian Man*—named for Marcus Vitruvius, the brilliant Roman architect who praised the *Divine Proportion* in his text *De Architectura*.

"Nobody understood better than Da Vinci the divine structure of the human body. Da Vinci actually *exhumed* corpses to measure the exact proportions of human bone structure. He was the first to show that the human body is literally made of building blocks whose proportional ratios *always* equal PHI."

Everyone in class gave him a dubious look.

"Don't believe me?" Langdon challenged. "Next time you're in the shower, take a tape measure."

A couple of football players snickered.

"Not just you insecure jocks," Langdon prompted. "All of you. Guys and girls. Try it. Measure the distance from the tip of your head to the floor. Then divide that by the distance from your belly button to the floor. Guess what number you get."

"Not PHI!" one of the jocks blurted out in disbelief.

"Yes, PHI," Langdon replied. "One-point-six-one-eight. Want another example? Measure the distance from your shoulder to your fingertips, and then divide it by the distance from your elbow to your fingertips. PHI again. Another? Hip to floor divided by knee to floor. PHI again. Finger joints. Toes. Spinal divisions. PHI. PHI. PHI. My friends, each of you is a walking tribute to the Divine Proportion."

. . .

Over the next half hour, Langdon showed them slides of artwork by Michelangelo, Albrecht Dürer, Da Vinci, and many others, demonstrating each artist's intentional and rigorous adherence to the Divine Proportion in the layout of his compositions. Langdon unveiled PHI in the architectural dimensions of the Greek Parthenon, the pyramids of Egypt, and even the United Nations Building in New York. PHI appeared in the organizational structures of Mozart's sonatas, Beethoven's Fifth Symphony, as well as the works of Bartók, Debussy, and Schubert. The number PHI, Langdon told them, was even used by Stradivarius to calculate the exact placement of the f-holes in the construction of his famous violins.

"In closing," Langdon said, walking to the chalkboard, "we return to *symbols*." He drew five intersecting lines that formed a five-pointed star. "This symbol is one of the most powerful images you will see this term. Formally known as a pentagram—or *pentacle*, as the ancients called it—this symbol is considered both divine and magical by many cultures. Can anyone tell me why that might be?"

Stettner, the math major, raised his hand. "Because if you draw a pentagram, the lines automatically divide themselves into segments according to the Divine Proportion."

Langdon gave the kid a proud nod. "Nice job. Yes, the ratios of line segments in a pentacle all equal PHI, making this symbol the ultimate expression of the Divine Proportion. For this reason, the five-pointed star has always been the symbol for beauty and perfection associated with the goddess and the sacred feminine."

The girls in class beamed.

"One note, folks. We've only touched on Da Vinci today, but we'll be seeing a lot more of him this semester. Leonardo was a well-documented devotee of the ancient ways of the goddess. Tomorrow, I'll show you his fresco *The Last Supper*, which is one of the most astonishing tributes to the sacred feminine you will ever see."

"You're kidding, right?" somebody said. "I thought *The Last Supper* was about Jesus!"

Langdon winked. "There are symbols hidden in places you would never imagine."

13 - 3 - 2 - 21 - 1 - 1 - 8 - 5

1 - 1 - 2 - 3 - 5 - 8 - 13 - 21

SANTA MARIA DELLE GRAZIE, MILAN

Sir Teabing's Lecture on The Last Supper

Teabing reached for the book and flipped toward the center.

. . .

"I assume you recognize this fresco?"

He's kidding, right? Sophie was staring at the most famous fresco of all time—*The Last Supper*—Da Vinci's legendary painting from the wall of Santa Maria delle Grazie in Milan. The decaying fresco portrayed Jesus and His disciples at the moment that Jesus announced one of them would betray Him. "I know the fresco, yes."

"Then perhaps you would indulge me this little game? Close your eyes if you would."

Uncertain, Sophie closed her eyes.

"Where is Jesus sitting?" Teabing asked.

"In the center."

"Good. And what food are He and His disciples breaking and eating?"

"Bread." *Obviously.*

"Superb. And what drink?"

"Wine. They drank wine."

"Great. And one final question. How many wine-glasses are on the table?"

Sophie paused, realizing it was the trick question. *And after dinner, Jesus took the cup of wine, sharing it with His disciples.* "One cup," she said. "The chalice." The Cup of Christ. The Holy Grail. "Jesus passed a single chalice of wine, just as modern Christians do at communion."

Teabing sighed. "Open your eyes."

She did. Teabing was grinning smugly. Sophie looked down at the painting, seeing to her astonishment that *everyone* at the table had a glass of wine, including Christ. Thirteen cups. Moreover, the cups were tiny, stemless, and made of glass. There was no chalice in the painting. No Holy Grail.

Teabing's eyes twinkled. "A bit strange, don't you think, considering that both the Bible and our standard Grail legend celebrate this moment as the definitive arrival of the Holy Grail. Oddly, Da Vinci appears to have forgotten to paint the Cup of Christ."

"Surely art scholars must have noted that."

"You will be shocked to learn what anomalies Da Vinci included here that most scholars either do not see or simply choose to ignore. This fresco, in fact, is the entire key to the Holy Grail mystery. Da Vinci lays it all out in the open in *The Last Supper.*"

Sophie scanned the work eagerly. "Does this fresco tell us what the Grail really is?"

"Not *what* it is," Teabing whispered. "But rather *who* it is. The Holy Grail is not a thing. It is, in fact . . . a *person*."

. . .

"Sophie, legend tells us the Holy Grail is a chalice—a cup. But the Grail's description as a *chalice* is actually an allegory to protect the true nature of the Holy Grail. That is to say, the legend uses the chalice as a metaphor for something far more important."

"A woman," Sophie said.

"Exactly." Langdon smiled. "The Grail is literally the ancient symbol for womanhood, and the *Holy* Grail represents the sacred feminine and the goddess, which of course has now been lost, virtually eliminated by the Church.

. . .

Sophie shook her head. "I'm sorry, when you said the Holy Grail was a person, I thought you meant it was an actual person."

"It is," Langdon said.

"And not just any person," Teabing blurted, clambering excitedly to his feet. "A woman who carried with her a secret so powerful that, if revealed, it threatened to devastate the very foundation of Christianity!"

Sophie looked overwhelmed. "Is this woman well known in history?"

"Quite." Teabing collected his crutches and motioned down the hall. "And if we adjourn to the study, my friends, it would be my honor to show you Da Vinci's painting of her."

Langdon smiled. "As it turns out, the Holy Grail does indeed make an appearance in *The Last Supper*. Leonardo included her prominently."

"Hold on," Sophie said. "You told me the Holy Grail is a *woman*. *The Last Supper* is a painting of thirteen men."

"Is it?" Teabing arched his eyebrows. "Take a closer look."

Uncertain, Sophie made her way closer to the painting, scanning the thirteen figures—Jesus Christ in the middle, six disciples on His left, and six on His right. "They're all men," she confirmed.

"Oh?" Teabing said. "How about the one seated in the place of honor, at the right hand of the Lord?"

Sophie examined the figure to Jesus' immediate right, focusing in. As she studied the person's face and body, a wave of astonishment rose within her. The individual had flowing red hair, delicate folded hands, and the hint of a bosom. It was, without a doubt . . . female.

"That's a woman!" Sophie exclaimed.

"That, my dear," Teabing replied, "is Mary Magdalene."

Sophie turned. "The prostitute?"

Teabing drew a short breath, as if the word had injured him personally. "Magdalene was no such thing.

That unfortunate misconception is the legacy of a smear campaign launched by the early Church. The Church needed to defame Mary Magdalene in order to cover up her dangerous secret—her role as the Holy Grail."

Sophie looked at him. "You're saying the Christian Church was to be carried on by a *woman?*"

"That was the plan. Jesus was the original feminist. He intended for the future of His Church to be in the hands of Mary Magdalene."

"And Peter had a problem with that," Langdon said, pointing to *The Last Supper.* "That's Peter there. You can see that Da Vinci was well aware of how Peter felt about Mary Magdalene."

Again, Sophie was speechless. In the painting, Peter was leaning menacingly toward Mary Magdalene and slicing his blade-like hand across her neck. The same threatening gesture as in *Madonna of the Rocks!*

"And here too," Langdon said, pointing now to the crowd of disciples near Peter. "A bit ominous, no?"

Sophie squinted and saw a hand emerging from the crowd of disciples. "Is that hand wielding a *dagger?*"

"Yes. Stranger still, if you count the arms, you'll see that this hand belongs to . . . no one at all. It's disembodied. Anonymous."

a photo from one of your
Da Vinci Code side trips here

THE OPUS DEI NATIONAL HEADQUARTERS, NEW YORK

Murray Hill Place—the new Opus Dei National Headquarters and conference center—is located at 243 Lexington Avenue in New York City. With a price tag of just over $47 million, the 133,000-square-foot tower is clad in red brick and Indiana limestone. Designed by May & Pinska, the building contains over one hundred bedrooms, six dining rooms, libraries, living rooms, meeting rooms, and offices. The second, eighth, and sixteenth floors contain chapels, ornamented with millwork and marble. The seventeenth floor is entirely residential.

"It is the mystery and wonderment THAT SERVE OUR SOULS, NOT THE GRAIL ITSELF. THE BEAUTY OF THE GRAIL LIES IN HER ETHEREAL NATURE." MARIE CHAUVEL GAZED UP AT ROSSLYN NOW. "FOR SOME, THE GRAIL IS A CHALICE THAT WILL BRING THEM EVERLASTING LIFE. FOR OTHERS, IT IS THE QUEST FOR LOST DOCUMENTS AND SECRET HISTORY. AND FOR MOST, I SUSPECT THE HOLY GRAIL IS SIMPLY A GRAND IDEA . . . A GLORIOUS UNATTAINABLE TREASURE THAT SOMEHOW, EVEN IN TODAY'S WORLD OF CHAOS, INSPIRES US."

CREDITS

Cover, pages 24, 29, 32: Mona Lisa, Louvre, Paris, France, Giraudon/Bridgeman Art Library

Cover, pages 19, 29, 138, 145: Vitruvian Man, Galleria dell'Accademia, Venice, Italy/Bridgeman Art Library

Cover and interior motif: Dead Sea Scrolls Foundation, Inc./ CORBIS

Page 1: Antique map of Paris, Historic Cities Research Project, http://historic-cities.huji.ac.il, The Hebrew University of Jerusalem, The Jewish National and University Library

Page 7, 21: Pyramid entrance to the Louvre, Taxi/Getty Images

Pages 8, 66, 78: Maps of Paris and London © 2004 by Fodor's LLC, a subsidiary of Random House, Inc.; cartography by David Lindroth

Page 10, 45: Color compass, Fotosearch

Page 10: Eiffel Tower, CORBIS

Page 15: Arc du Carrousel © David Henry, www.davidphenry.com

Page 16: Venus de Milo, Réunion des Musées Nationaux/Art Resource, NY

Page 25: Self-Portrait, Leonardo Da Vinci, Alinari/Art Resource, NY

Page 36,37: Madonna of the Rocks, Art Resource, NY

Page 55: Saint-Sulpice tower © David Henry, www.davidphenry.com

Page 57: Saint-Sulpice façade © Claude Boissy

Page 62: Château de Villette, photo courtesy of owner Olivia Hsu Decker, photographed by Pat Denton. For rental availability and information about Château Villette, please visit www.Frenchvacation.com or email Villette@Frenchvacation.com

Page 68: Arago Medallions © David Henry, www.davidphenry.com

Page 70: Pyramid Inversee © Linda Mathieu

Page 77: Temple Church © Simon Brighton

Page 83: Temple Church with column © David M. Lownie, www.crusader.org.uk

Page 84: Temple Church floor plan, illustration by Judith Stagnitto Abbate

Page 87: Effigy of Templar Knights, *The Temple Church,* C.G. Addison (1843), courtesy of David M. Lownie, www.crusader.org.uk

Page 92: Madonna of the Rocks (Virgin of the Rocks), Erich Lessing/ Art Resource, NY

Page 97: Big Ben, Workbook Stock

Page 99: Westminster Abbey, Westminster City Archives

Page 102: Sir Isaac Newton, Art Resource, NY

Page 103, 133: Codex Leicester, Leonardo Da Vinci, Seth Joel/CORBIS

Page 105: Chapter House of Westminster Abbey, Angelo Hornak/CORBIS

Pages 109, 116, 118, 120, 123: Rosslyn Chapel photographs, © Antonia Reeve/Rosslyn Chapel Trust

Page 110: Rosslyn Chapel floor plan, Rosslyn Chapel Trust

Page 129, 146, 147, 150, 151: The Last Supper, Scala/Art Resource, NY

Page 131: Castel Gandolfo, Specola Vaticana, Veduta/Vasari

Page 135: Pentacle sketch, Laura Palese